BELLA-VISTA

COLETTE

Bella-Vista

Translated by Antonia White

Preface Translated by Matthew Ward

THE MODERN LIBRARY

NEW YORK

1996 Modern Library Edition

Translation copyright © 1958 by Martin Secker and Warburg,
Ltd. Copyright renewed 1986 by Farrar, Straus and Giroux,
Incorporated.
Preface translation copyright © 1983 by Farrar, Straus and
Giraux, Incorporated.

Library of Congress Cataloging-in-Publication Data
Colette, 1873–1954.
[Bella-vista. English]
Bella-vista/Colette; translated by Antonia White;
with a preface translated by Matthew Ward.
p. cm.
ISBN 0-679-77097-6
I. White, Antonia, 1899– . II. Title.
PQ2605.O28B413 1996 843′.912—dc20 95-42529

Manufactured in the United States of America
2 4 6 8 9 7 5 3 1

PREFACE

No real place served as model for Bella-Vista, a small Provençale inn, which I painted to resemble twenty imitation farmhouses planted on a notch on the Mediterranean, draped, in one season, with plumbago, passion flower, and those convolvulus, bluer than the day, whose teeming avidity I measured against pink walls. Bella-Vista is any chimera of those who, leaving the heart of a dense and exhausting city, demand daily sun, undisturbed good weather, and constant heat. Until I found out for myself that good weather is another chimera and another kind of exhaustion, the region around St.-Tropez gave me all I asked for in the way of daily splendor. I was only just discovering it at the time I was writing "Bella-Vista." With no domain of my own on its shore, I clung to this or that auberge, some Gulf hotel; I didn't realize that the little port into which the dog, the cock, and the saint sailed had, strangely enough, but one access road, a single entrance, like a lobster pot. So that, fifteen years later, I was still moored to this little peninsula jutting out into the sea. At twilight it appears suspended there, the color of lilacs, looking like new steel beneath the full moon; dawn makes all the walls that face east blush briefly with a powdery pink, whereas, before sunrise, the thick vineyard is but a crimped blackness.

There, or thereabouts, is where my knowledge of Provence ends. In fifteen years I moved very little. From St.-Tropez to Fréjus, from Pampelonne to Thoronet, from a rosé wine to a golden wine, from ailloli to pissaladière, from one dawn to one night snowy with stars . . . it is enough to remember, enough to be thankful for . . . The prudent weariness of age keeps me from running any risk of forgetting that a sovereign blue color weighs down on the imaginary rooftops of Bella-Vista, or that the west wind rises fresh toward noon, or that sleep, in the breezy shade, is conducive to dreaming and speaks, to the trusting sleeper, of motionless ships and islands free from danger.

[Translated by Matthew Ward]

BELLA-VISTA

BELLA VISTA

It is absurd to suppose that periods empty of love are blank pages in a woman's life. The truth is just the reverse. What remains to be said about a passionate love affair? It can be told in three lines. *He* loved me, I loved *Him*. His presence obliterated all other presences. We were happy. Then *He* stopped loving me and I suffered.

Frankly, the rest is eloquence or mere verbiage. When a love affair is over, there comes a lull during which one is once more aware of friends and passersby, of things constantly happening as they do in a vivid, crowded dream. Once again, one is conscious of normal feelings such as fear, gaiety, and boredom; once again time exists and one registers its flight. When I was younger, I did not realize the importance of these "blank pages." The anecdotes with which they furnished me—those impassioned, misguided, simple, or inscrutable human beings who plucked me by the sleeve, made me their witness for a moment, and then let me go—provided more "romantic" subjects than my private personal drama. I shall not finish my task as a writer without attempting, as I want to do here, to draw them out of the shadows to which the shameless necessity of speaking of love in my own name has consigned them.

A house, even a very small house, does not make itself habitable or adopt us in the week which follows the signing of the agreement. As a wise man of few words who makes sandals at St.-Tropez once said: "It takes as much work and thought to make sandals for someone aged six as to make them for someone aged forty."

Thirteen years ago when I bought a small vineyard beside the sea of the South of France with its plumy pines, its mimosas and its little house, I regarded them with the prompt business-like eye of a camper. "I'll unpack my two suitcases; I'll put the bathtub and the portable shower in a corner, the Breton table and its armchair under the window, the divan-bed and its mosquito net in the dark room. I'll sleep *there* and I'll work *there* and I'll wash *there*. By tomorrow, everything will be ready." For the dining room, I could choose between the shade of the mulberry and that of the centuries-old spindle trees.

Having the necessities—that is to say shade, sun, roses, sea, a well, and a vine—I had a healthy contempt for such luxuries as electricity, a kitchen stove, and a pump. More prudent influences seduced me from leaving the little Provençal house in its primitive perfection. I gave in to them and listened to the convincing builder whom I went to see in his own home.

He was smiling. In his garden an all-the-year-round mimosa and purple wallflowers set off to advantage the various objects for sale: concrete benches, upended balusters arranged like skittles, drain pipes, and perforated bricks, the lot under the guardianship of a very pretty bulldog in turquoise Vallauris ware.

"You know how things are here," said the builder. "If you need your villa by July or August, you'll have to come and bully the workman on his own ground now and then."

I remember that I kept blinking my eyelids, which were hurt by the chalky glare of March. The sky was patterned with great white clouds and the mistral was shaking all the doors in their frames. It was cold under the table but a sunbeam, which fell on the estimate covered with red figures and black dots and blue pencil ticks, burned the back of my hand. I caught myself thinking that warm rain is very agreeable in spring in the Ile-de-France and that a heated, draft-proof flat in Paris, staked out with lamps under parchment hats, has an unrivaled charm.

The Midi triumphed. I had indeed just been having

attack after attack of bronchitis and the words "warm climate . . . rest . . . open air . . ." became the accomplices of the smiling builder. I decided therefore to try to find a haven of rest, some way away from the port to which I have since become so deeply attached, from which I could sally forth from time to time to "bully the workmen." This would give me an excuse to escape from the most exhausting of all pleasures, conversation.

Thanks to a decorative painter who takes his holidays alone and makes himself unrecognizable, in the manner of Greta Garbo, by wearing sunglasses and sleeveless tennis shirts, I learned that a certain inn, crowded with odd people in the summer but peaceful for the rest of the year, would take me under its roof. I call it Bella-Vista because there are as many Bella-Vistas and Vista-Bellas in France as there are Montignys. You will not find it on the Mediterranean coast; it has lost its proprietresses and nearly all its charms. It has even lost its old name, which I shall not reveal.

Consequently, at the end of March, I packed a good pound of periwinkle-blue paper in a suitcase. I also put in my heavy wool slacks, my four pullovers, some woolen scarves, and my tartan-lined mackintosh—all the necessary equipment, in short, for winter sports or an expedition to the Pole. My previous stays in the Midi, during a lecture tour at the end of one winter, called up memories of Cannes blind with hail and Marseilles and Toulon as white and gritty as cuttlefish bones under the January mistral. They also evoked bright blue and pale green landscapes, followed by grim recollections of leeches and injections of camphorated oil.

These discouraging images accompanied me almost to the "hostelry" I call Bella-Vista. Concerning Bella-Vista I shall give only certain inoffensive details and draw posthumous portraits such as those of its two proprietresses of whom one, the younger, is dead. Supposing the other to be alive, heaven knows on what work, and in what place of seclusion, those agile fingers and piercing eyes are now employed.

Thirteen years ago, the two of them stood in the doorway of Bella-Vista. One expertly seized my smooth-haired griffon by the loose skin of her neck and back, deposited her on the ground, and said to her: "Hello, dear little yellow dog. I'm sure you is thirsty."

The other held out her firm hand, with its big ring, to help me out of the car and greeted me by name: "A quarter of an hour later, Madame Colette, and you'd have missed it."

"Missed what?"

"The *bourride*. They wouldn't have left you a mouthful. I know them. Madame Ruby, when you can take your mind for one moment off that dog."

Her charming accent took one straight back to the

Place Blanche. She had acquired the red, uneven sun-
burn peculiar to high-colored blondes. Her dyed hair
showed grayish at the roots; there was spontaneous
laughter in her bright blue eyes and her teeth were
still splendid. Her tailored white linen dress glistened
from repeated ironing. A striking person, in fact; one
of those who make an instant, detailed physical impression. Before I had even spoken to her, I already
knew by heart the pleasant shape of her hands baked
by the sun and much cooking, her gold signet ring,
her small wide-nostriled nose, her piercing glance
which plunged straight into one's own eyes, and the
good smell of laundered linen, thyme, and garlic
which almost drowned her Paris scent.

"Madame Suzanne," retorted her American partner, "you is lost in Madame Colette's opinion if you
is nicer to her than to her little yellow dog."

Having made this statement, Madame Ruby announced lunch by ringing a little copper bell whose
angry voice quite unhinged my griffon bitch. Instead
of obeying the bell, I remained standing in the courtyard, a square which, like a stage set, lacked one
side. Perched on a modest eminence, Bella-Vista pru-
dently turned its back to the sea and offered its façade
and its two wings to the kindly winds, contenting
itself with a restricted view. From its paved terrace I
discovered in turn the forest, some sheltered fields,
and a dark blue fragment of the Mediterranean
wedged between two slopes of hills.

"You isn't any other luggage?"

"The suitcase, my dressing case, the carry-all, the rug. That's all, Madame Ruby."

At the sound of her name, she gave me a familiar smile. Then she called a dark-haired servant girl and showed her my luggage.

"Room 10!"

But though room 10, on the first floor, looked out on the sea, it refused me my favorite southwest aspect. So I chose instead a room on the ground floor which opened directly onto the terrace courtyard. It was opposite the garage and not far from the aviary of parakeets.

"Here you is more noisy," objected Madame Ruby. "The garage . . ."

"It's empty, thank heaven."

"Quite right. Our car sleeps outdoors. It's more convenient than going in, coming out, going in, coming out. So, you likes number 4 better?"

"I do like it better."

"O.K. Here's the bath, here's the light, here's the bell, here's the cupboards"—she swept up my dog and threw her deftly onto the flowered counterpane—"and here's yellow dog!"

The bitch laughed with pleasure while Madame Ruby, enchanted with the effect she had produced, pivoted on her rubber soles. I watched her cross the courtyard and thought that, from head to foot, she was exactly as she had been described to me. She was scandalous, but one liked her at first sight. She was mannish without being awkward, her boy's hips and square shoulders were trimly encased in blue frieze and white linen; there was a rose in the lapel of her jacket. Her head was round and could not have been more beautifully modeled under the smooth cap of red hair. It had lost its golden glint and showed white in places and she wore it plastered to her skull with severe, provocative coquetry. There was something definitely attractive about her wide gray eyes, her unassuming nose, her big mouth with its big, seemingly indestructible teeth, and her skin, which was freckled over the cheekbones. Forty-five perhaps? More like fifty. The neck in the open cellular shirt was thickening and the loose skin and prominent veins on the back of the strong hands revealed that she might well be even more than fifty.

Undoubtedly I cannot draw Madame Ruby as well as I heard Madame Suzanne describe her later in a moment of irritation.

"You look like an English curate! You're the living image of a Boche got up as a sportsman! You're the living image of a vicious governess! Oh, I know you were an American schoolteacher! But I'd no more have trusted you with my little sister's education than my little brother's!"

On the day of my arrival, I still knew very little about the two friends who ran Bella-Vista. A sense of well-being, unforeseen rather than anticipated, descended on me and kept me standing there with my arms crossed on the windowsill of room 4. I submitted myself passively to the reverberations of the yellow walls and blue shutters; I forgot my exacting griffon bitch, my own hunger, and the meal now in progress. In that odd state of convalescence which follows a tiring night journey, my eyes wandered slowly around the courtyard. They came to rest on the rosebush under my window, idly following every sway of its branches. "Roses already! And white arum lilies. The wisteria's beginning to come out. And all those black-and-yellow pansies."

A long dog, lying stretched out in the courtyard, had wagged its tail as Madame Ruby passed. A white pigeon had come and pecked at the toes of her white shoes . . . From the aviary came a gentle, muffled screeching: the soft, monotonous language of the green parakeets. And I was glad that my unknown room behind me was filled with the smell of lavender, dry bunches of which were hung on the bed rail and in the cupboard.

The duty of having to examine them poisons one's pleasure in new places. I dreaded the dining room as if I were a traveler contemplating the panorama of an unknown town and thinking: "What a nuisance that I'll have to visit two museums, the cathedral, and the docks." For nothing will give the traveler as much pleasure as that warm rampart or that little cemetery or those old dikes covered with grass and ivy . . . and the stillness.

"Come along, Pati."

The griffon followed me with dignity because I had only said her name once. She was called Pati when it was necessary for us both to be on our best behavior. When it was time for her walk, she was Pati-Pati-Pati, or as many more Patis as one had breath to add. Thus we had adapted her name to all the essential circumstances of our life. In the same way, when Madame Ruby spoke French, she contented herself with the single auxiliary verb "to be" which stood for all the others: "You is all you want? . . . You is no more luggage?" and so on. As I crossed the court-yard, I had already assigned Madame Ruby to that category of active, rather limited people who easily learn the nouns and adjectives of a foreign language but jib at verbs and their conjugation.

The prostrate dog half hitched himself up for Pati's benefit. She pretended to ignore his existence, and by degrees, he collapsed again: first his shoulders; then his neck, which was too thin; lastly his mongrel grey-hound's head, which was too large. A brisk, rather chilly breeze was blowing wallflower petals over the sand but I was grateful to feel the bite of the sun on my shoulder. Over the wall, an invisible garden wafted the scent which demoralizes the bravest, the smell of orange trees in flower.

In the dining room, which was far from monumental but low-ceilinged and carefully shaded, a dozen small scattered tables with coarse Basque linen cloths reassured my unsociable disposition. There was no butter in shells, no headwaiter in greenish-black tails and none of those meager vases containing one marguerite, one tired anemone, and one spray of mimosa. But there was a big square of ice-cool butter and on the folded napkin lay a rose from the climbing rose tree: a single rose whose lips were a little harsh from the mistral and the salt; a rose I was free to pin to my sweater or to eat as an hors-d'œuvre. I directed a smile toward the presiding goddesses, but the smile missed its target. Madame Ruby, alone at a table, was hurrying through her meal and only Madame Suzanne's bust was visible. Every time the kitchen hatch opened, her golden hair and her hot face appeared in its frame against a background of shining saucepans and gridirons. Pati and I had the famous *bourride*, velvet-smooth and generously laced with garlic; a large helping of roast pork stuffed with sage and served with applesauce and potatoes; cheese, stewed pears flavored with vanilla, and a small carafe of the local *vin rosé*. I foresaw that three weeks of such food would repair the ravages of two attacks of bronchitis. When the coffee was poured out—it was quite ordinary coffee but admirably hot—Madame Ruby came over and vainly offered me her cigarette lighter.

"You is not a smoker? O.K."

She showed her tact by going off at once to her duties and not prolonging the conversation. As she moved away, I admired her rhythmic, swaying walk.

My griffon bitch sat opposite me in the depths of a knitted woolen hood I had presented to her. For correct deportment and silence at table, she could have given points to an English child. The restraint was not entirely disinterested. She knew that the perfection of her behavior would not only win her general approval but more concrete tributes of esteem such as lumps of sugar soaked in coffee and morsels of cake. To this end she gave a tremendous display of engaging head turnings, expressive glances, false modesty, affected gravity, and all the terrier airs and graces. A kind of military salute invented by herself—the front paw raised to the level of the ear—which one might call the C in alt of her gamut of tricks, provoked laughter and delighted exclamations. I have to admit that she occasionally overdid this playing to the gallery.

I have written elsewhere of this tiny bitch, a sporting dog in miniature with a deep chest, cropped ears like little horns, and the soundest of health and intelligence. Like certain dogs with round skulls—bulldogs, griffons, and Pekinese—she "worked" on her own. She learned words by the dozen and was always observant and on the alert. She registered sounds and never failed to attribute the right meaning to them. She possessed a "rule of the road" which varied according to whether we were traveling by train or by car. Brought up in Belgium in the company of horses, she passionately followed everything that wore iron shoes for the pleasure of running behind them and she knew how to avoid being kicked.

She was artful; a born liar and pretender. Once, in Brittany, I saw her give a splendid imitation of a poor, brave, suffering little dog with its cheek all swollen from a wasp sting. But two could play at that game and I gave her a slap which made her spit out her swelling. It was a ball of dried donkey's dung which she had stowed away in her cheek so as to bring it home and enjoy it at leisure.

Glutted with food and less overcome with fatigue than I was, Pati sat up straight on the other side of the table and took an inventory of the people and things about us. There was a lady and her daughter, who appeared to be the same age: the daughter was already decrepit and the mother still looked young. There were two boys on their Easter holidays who asked for more bread at every course, and finally, there was a solitary resident, sitting not far from us, who seemed to me quite unremarkable though he riveted Pati's attention. Twice, when he was speaking to the dark-haired maid, she puffed out her lips to snarl something offensive and then thought better of it.

I did not scold myself for sitting on there, with the remains of my coffee cooling in my cup, glancing now at the swaying rosebush, now at the yellow walls and the copies of English prints. I stared at the sunlit courtyard, then at something else, then at nothing at all. When I drift like that, completely slack, it is a sign not that I am bored but that all my forces are silently coalescing and that I am floating like a seed on the wind. It is a sign that, out of wisps and stray threads and scattered straws, I am fashioning for myself just one more fragment of a kind of youth. "Suppose I go and sleep? . . . Suppose I go and look at the sea? . . . Suppose I send a telegram to Paris? . . . Suppose I telephone to the builder?"

The resident who had not the luck to please my dog said something to the dark-haired girl as he got up. She answered: "In a moment, Monsieur Daste." He passed close by my table, gave a vague apologetic bow, and said something like "Huisipisi" to my dog in a jocular way. At this she put up her hackles till she looked like a bottle brush and tried to bite his hand.

"Pati! Are you crazy? She's not bad-tempered," I said to Monsieur Daste. "Just rather conventional. She doesn't know you."

"Yes, yes, she knows me all right. She knows me all right," muttered Monsieur Daste.

He bent toward the dog and threatened her teasingly with his forefinger. Pati showed that she did not much relish being treated like a fractious child. I held her back while Monsieur Daste moved away, laughing under his breath. Now that I looked at him more attentively, I saw that he was a rather short, nimble man who gave a general impression of a grayness: gray suit, gray hair, and a grayish tinge in his small-featured face. I had already noticed his tapering forefinger and its polished nail. The dog growled something that was obviously insulting.

"Look here," I told her. "You've got to get used to the idea that you're not in your own village of Auteuil. There here are dogs, birds, possibly hens, rabbits, and even cats. You're got to accept them. Now, let's take a turn."

At that moment Madame Suzanne came and sat down to her well-earned meal.

"Well? How was the lunch?" she called to me from her distant table.

"Perfect, Madame Suzanne. I could do with one meal like that every day—but only one! Now we're going to take a turn around the house to walk it off a little."

"What about a siesta?"

"Everything in its own good time. I'm never sleepy the first day."

Her plump person had the effect of making me talk in proverbs and maxims and all the facile clichés of "popular" wisdom.

"Will the fine weather hold, Madame Suzanne?"

She powdered her face, ran a moistened finger over

her eyebrows, and made her table napkin crack like a whip as she unfolded it.

"There's a bit of east wind. Here it rains if there isn't a touch of wind."

She made a face as she emptied the hard-boiled-egg salad out of the hors-d'œuvres dish onto her plate.

"As to the *bourride,* I'll have to do without, as usual. I don't care—I licked out the bowl I made the sauce in."

Her laugh irradiated her face. Looking at her I thought that, before thin females became the fashion, it was the fair-haired Madame Suzannes with their high color and high breasts who were the beautiful women.

"You take a hand in the kitchen every day, Madame Suzanne?"

"Oh, I like it, you know. In Paris I kept a little restaurant. You never came and ate my chicken with rice on a Saturday night in the rue Lepic? I'll make one for you. But what a bloody hell of a place—excuse my language—this part of France is for provisions."

"What about the early vegetables?"

"Early vegetables! Don't make me laugh. Everything's later here than it is in Brittany. Some little lettuces you can hardly see . . . a few beans. The artichokes are hardly beginning. No tomatoes before June except the Spanish and Italian ones. In winter, except for their rotten oranges, almonds, raisins, nuts, and figs are all we get in the way of fruit. As to new-laid eggs, you've got to fight for them. And when it comes to fish! . . . The weekly boarders in hotels are the luckiest. At least they pay a fixed price and know where they are.''

She laughed and rubbed her hands together; those hands which had been tried and proven by every sort and kind of work.

''I love the kitchen stove. I'm not like Madame Ruby. Lucie!'' she called toward the hatch. ''Bring me the pork and a little of the pears! Madame Ruby,'' she went on, with ironic respect, ''cooking's not *her* affair. Oh dear, no! Nor is managing things and doing the accounts. Oh dear, no!''

She dropped the mockery and emphasized the respect.

''No, her affair is *chic*, manners and so on. Furnishing a room, arranging a table, receiving a guest —she's a born genius at all that. I admit it and I appreciate it. I really do appreciate it. But . . .''

An angry little spark animated Madame Suzanne's blue eyes.

''But I can't stand seeing her wandering all over the kitchen, lifting up the saucepan lids and throwing her weight about. 'Madame Suzanne, do you know you is made coffee like dishwater this morning? Lucie, you is not forgotten to fill the ice trays in the refrigerator?' No, that's really *too* much!''

She imitated to perfection her friend's voice and

her peculiar grammar. Flushed with an apparently childish jealousy and irritation, she seemed not to mind in the least revealing or underlining what people called the "strange intimacy" which bound her to her partner. She changed her tone as she saw Lucie approaching. Lucie had a succulent, foolish mouth and a great mass of turbulent black hair which curled at the nape of her neck.

"Madame Colette, I'm making a special *crème caramel* tonight for Monsieur Daste. I'll make a little extra if you'd like it. Monsieur Daste only likes sweet things and red meat."

"And who is Monsieur Daste?"

"A very nice man . . . I believe what I see. It's the best way, don't you think? He's all on his own, for one thing. So he's almost certainly a bachelor. Have you seen him, by the way?"

"Only a glimpse."

"He's a man who plays bridge and poker. And he's awfully well educated, you know."

"Is this an insidious proposal of marriage, Madame Suzanne?"

She got up and slapped me on the shoulder.

"Ah, anyone can see you're artistic. You still talk the way artistic people do. I'm going to have half an hour's nap. You see *I* get up every morning at half past five."

"You've hardly eaten anything, Madame Suzanne."

"It'll make me slimmer."

She frowned, yawned, and then lifted one of the coarse red net curtains.

"Where's that Ruby run off to now? Will you excuse me, Madame Colette? If I'm not everywhere at once . . ."

She left me planted there and I invited my dog to come for a walk around the hotel. A sharp wind enveloped us as soon as we set foot on the terrace but the sun was still on the little flight of steps leading up to my french window and on the aviary of parakeets. The birds were billing and cooing in couples and playing hide-and-seek in their still empty birchbark nests. At the foot of the aviary, a white rabbit was sunning himself. He did not run away and gave my griffon such a warlike glance with his red eye that she went some way off and relieved herself to keep herself in countenance.

Beyond the walls of the courtyard, the wind was having everything its own way. Pati flattened her ears and I should have gone back to my room if, quite close, shut in between two hillocks of forest, I had not caught sight of the Mediterranean.

At that time I had only a rudimentary acquaintance with the Mediterranean. Compared to the low tides of Brittany and that damp, pungent air, this bluest and saltiest of seas, so decorative and so unchangeable, meant little to me. But merely sniffing it from afar made the griffon's snub nose turn moist and there was nothing for it but to follow Pati to the foot of a little scarp covered with evergreens. There was no beach; only some flat rocks between which seaweed, with spreading branches like a peacock's tail, waved gently just below the surface of the water.

The valorous griffon wet her paws, tested the water, approved of it, sneezed several times, and began to hunt for her Breton crabs. But no waves provide less game than those which wash the southern coast and she had to restrict herself to the pleasure of exploring. She ran from tamarisk to lentiscus, from agave to myrtle, till she came on a man sitting under some low branches. As she growled insultingly at him, I guessed that it must be Monsieur Daste. He was laughing at her, wagging his forefinger, and saying: "Huisipisi"—doing everything, in fact, calculated to offend a very small, arrogant dog who was eager for admiring attention.

When I had called her back, Monsieur Daste made an apologetic gesture for not standing up and silently pointed to a treetop. I jerked my chin up questioningly.

"Wood pigeons," he said. "I think they're going to build their nest there. And there's another pair at the end of the kitchen garden at Bella-Vista."

"You're not thinking of shooting them, are you?"

He threw up his hands in protest.

"Shooting? Me? Good Lord! You'll never see *me* carrying a gun. But I watch them. I listen to them."

He shut his eyes amorously like a music fiend at a concert. I took advantage of this to have a good look at him. He was neither ugly nor deformed; only rather mediocre. He seemed to have been made to attract as little attention as possible. His hair was thick and white and was as plentifully and evenly sprinkled among brown as in a roan horse's hide. His features were decidedly small; he had a stingy face which looked all the more stingy when the long eyelids were closed. If I observed Monsieur Daste more carefully than he deserved, it was because I am always terrified, when chance throws me among unknown people, of discovering some monstrosity in them. I search them to the core with a sharp, distasteful eye as one does a dressing-table drawer in a hotel bedroom. No old dressings? No hairpins, no broken buttons, no crumbs of tobacco? Then I breathe again and don't give it another thought.

In the pitiless light of two in the afternoon, Monsieur Daste, medium-sized, clean, and slightly desiccated, showed no visible signs of lupus or eczema. I could hardly hold it against him that he wore a soft white shirt and a neat tie instead of a pullover. I became affable.

"Pati, say how d'you do to Monsieur Daste."

I lifted the dog by her superfluous skin—nature provides the thoroughbred griffon with enough skin to clothe about a dog and a half—and held her over my arm for Monsieur Daste to appreciate the little squashed muzzle, the blackish-brown mask, and the beautiful prominent gold-flecked eyes. Pati did not try to bite Monsieur Daste, but I was surprised to feel her stiffen slightly.

"Pati, give your paw to Monsieur Daste."

She obeyed, but with her eyes elsewhere. She held out a limp, expressionless paw which Monsieur Daste shook in a sophisticated way.

"Are you in this part of the world for some time, Madame?"

As he had a pleasant voice, I gave Monsieur Daste some brief scraps of information.

"We wretched bureaucrats," he rejoined, "have the choice between three weeks' holiday at Easter or three in July. I need warmth. Bella-Vista is sheltered from the cold winds. But I find the very bright light distressing."

"Madame Suzanne is making you a *crème caramel* for tonight. You see what a lot of things I know already!"

Monsieur Daste closed his eyes.

"Madame Suzanne has all the virtues—even though appearances might lead one to suppose just the opposite."

"Really?"

"I can't help laughing," said Monsieur Daste. "Even if Madame Suzanne practices virtue, she hasn't any respect for it."

I thought he was going to run down our hostesses. I waited for the "They're impossible" I had heard *ad nauseam* in Paris to put an end to our conversation. But he merely raised his small hand like a preacher and remarked: "What are appearances, Madame, what are appearances?"

His chestnut-colored eyes stared thoughtfully at the empty sea, over which the shadows of the white clouds skimmed in dark green patches. I sat down on the dried seaweed that had been torn from the sea and piled up in heaps by the last gales of the equinox and my dog nestled quietly against my skirt. The sulphurous smell of the seaweed, the broken shells, the feeble waves which rose and fell without advancing or retreating gave me a sudden terrible longing for Brittany. I longed for its tides, for the great rollers off St.-Malo which rush in from the ocean, imprisoning constellations of starfish and jellyfish and hermit crabs in the heart of each greenish wave. I longed for the swift incoming tide with its plumes of spray; the tide which revived the thirsty mussels and the little rock oysters and reopened the cups of the sea anemones. The Mediterranean is not the sea.

A sharp gesture from Monsieur Daste distracted me from my homesickness.

"What is it?"

"Bird," said Monsieur Daste laconically.

"What bird?"

"I . . . I don't know. I didn't have time to make it out. But it was a big bird."

"And where are your wood pigeons?"

"My wood pigeons? Not *mine,* alas," he said regretfully.

He pointed to the little wood behind us.

"They were over there. They'll come back. So shall I. That slate-blue, that delicate fawn of their feathers when they spread them out in flight like a fan . . . Coo . . . croo-oo-oo . . . Coo . . . croo-oo-oo," he cooed, puffing out his chest and half closing his eyes.

"You are a poet, Monsieur Daste."

He opened his eyes, surprised.

"A poet . . ." he repeated. "Yes . . . a poet. That's exactly what I am, Madame. I must be, if *you* say so."

A few moments later Monsieur Daste left me, with obvious tact, on the pretext of "some letters to write." He set off in the direction of Bella-Vista with the short, light step of a good walker. Before he went, he did not omit to stick out his forefinger at Pati and to hiss "Huisipisi" at her. But she seemed to expect this teasing and did not utter a sound.

The two of us wandered alone along a beaten track which ran beside the sea at the edge of the forest which was thick with pines, lentiscus, and cork oaks. While I was scratching my fingers trying to pick some long-thorned broom and blue salvia and limp-petaled rock roses for my room, I was suddenly overcome with irresistible sleepiness. The sunshine became a burden and we hurried back up the green scarp.

Three beautiful old mulberry trees, long since tamed and cut into umbrella shapes, did not yet hide the back side of Bella-Vista. Mulberry leaves grow fast but they take a long time to pierce the seamed bark. The trees and the façade looked to me crabbed and harsh; there is a certain time in the afternoon when everything seems repellent to me. All that I longed to do was to shut myself away as soon as possible and the dog felt the same.

Already I no longer liked my room, although it was predominantly pink and red. Where could I plug in a lamp to light the table where I meant to work? I rang for the dark-haired Lucie, who brought me a bunch of white pinks which smelled slightly of creosote. She did not fix anything but went off to find Madame Ruby in person. The American winked one of her gray eyes, summed up the situation, and disappeared. When she returned, she was carrying a lamp with a green china shade, some cord, and a collection of tools. She sat sideways on the edge of the table and set to work with the utmost expertise, her cigarette stuck in the corner of her mouth. I watched her large, deft hands, her brisk, efficient movements, and the beautiful shape of her head, hardly spoiled by the thickening nape, under the faded red hair.

"Madame Ruby, you must be amazingly good with your hands."

She winked at me through the smoke.

"Have you traveled a lot?"

"All over the place . . . Excuse my cigarette."

She jumped down and tested the switch of the lamp.

"There. Is light for you to work?"

"Perfect! Bravo, the electrician!"

"The electrician's an old jack-of-all-trades. Will you sign one of your books for me?"

"Whenever you like. For . . . ?"

"For Miss Ruby Cooney. C . . . double o-n-e-y. Thank you."

I would gladly have stopped her going but I dared not display my curiosity. She rolled up her little tool kit, swept a few iron filings off the table with her hand, and went out, raising two fingers to the level of her ear with the careless ease of a mechanic.

———

Sleep is good at any time but not waking. A late March twilight, a hotel bedroom that I had forgotten while I slept, two gaping suitcases still unpacked. "Suppose I went away?" . . . The noise a bent finger makes rapping three times on a thin door is neither pleasant nor reassuring.

"Come in!"

But it was only a telegram: a few secret, affectionate words in the code a tender friendship had invented. Everything was all right. There was nothing to worry about. Pati was tearing up the blue telegram; the suitcases would only take a quarter of an hour to unpack; the water was hot; the bath filled quite quickly.

I took into the dining room one of those stout notebooks in which we mean to write down what positively must not be put off or forgotten. I meant to start "bullying the workmen" the very next day. Lucie ladled me out a large bowl of fish soup with spaghetti floating in it and inquired whether I had anything against "eggs . . . you know, dropped in the dish and the cheese put on top" and half a guinea fowl before the *crème caramel*.

By the end of dinner, all I had entered in the new notebook was "Buy a folding rule." But I had done honor to the excellent meal. My dog, stimulated by it, sparkled with gaiety. She smiled at Madame Ruby, alone at her table at the far end of the room, and pretended to ignore the presence of Monsieur Daste. Either the young mother or the old daughter was coughing behind me. The two athletic boys were overcome by the weariness which rewarded their energetic effort. "Just think," Lucie confided to me, "they've walked right around the headland. Twenty

miles, they've done!'' From where I sat, I could smell
the eau de Cologne of which they both reeked. Plan-
ning to shorten my stay, I wrote in the big notebook:
''Buy a small notebook.''

''You is seen the drawing room, Madame Colette?''

''Not yet, Madame Ruby. But tonight, I have to
admit that . . .''

''You'd like Lucie to bring you a hot drink in the
drawing room?''

I gave in, especially as Madame Ruby was already
holding my dear little yellow dog under her arm and
Pati was surreptitiously licking her ear, hoping I did
not notice. The drawing room looked out on the sea
and contained an upright piano, cane furniture, and
comfortable imitations of English armchairs. Remem-
bering that my room was almost next door, I eyed the
piano apprehensively. Madame Ruby winked.

''You likes music?''

Her quick deft hands lifted the lid of the piano,
opened its front, and disclosed bottles and cocktail
shakers.

''My idea. I did it all by myself. Gutted the piano
like a chicken. You likes some drink? No?''

She poured herself out a glass of brandy and swallowed it carelessly, as if in a hurry. Lucie brought me
one of those *tisanes* which will never convince me
that they deserve their reputation for being soothing
or digestive.

"Where is Madame Suzanne?" Madame Ruby asked Lucie in a restrained voice.

"Madame Suzanne is finishing the *boeuf à la mode* for tomorrow. She's just straining out the juice."

"O.K. Leave the tray. And give me an ashtray. You is too much bits of hair on your neck, my girl!"

Her big, energetic hand brushed the black bush of hair which frizzed on Lucie's nape. The girl trembled, nearly knocked over my full cup, and hurried out of the room.

Far from avoiding my look, Madame Ruby's own took on a victorious malice which drew attention to Lucie's distress so indiscreetly that, for the moment, I ceased to find the boyish woman sympathetic. I am eccentric enough to be repelled when love, whether abnormal or normal, imposes itself on the onlooker's attention or imagination. Madame Ruby was wise enough not to insist further and went over to the two worn-out boys to ask them if they wanted a liqueur. Her manly ease must have terrified them, for they beat a hasty retreat after having asked whether they could do "a spot of canoeing" the next day.

"Canoe? . . . I told them: 'We is not a Suicides' Club here!' "

She lifted the net curtain from the black windowpane. But in the darkness, only the bark of the mulberry trees and their sparse, luminously green new leaves showed in the beam of light from the room.

"By the way, Madame Ruby . . . When you're

shopping tomorrow, will you go to Sixte's and get us some more breakfast cups? The same kind, the red-and-white ones.''

Madame Suzanne was behind us, still hot from coping with the dinner and the *boeuf à la mode,* but neat, dressed in white linen, freshly powdered, and smelling almost too good. I found her pleasing from head to foot. She felt my cordiality and returned me smile for smile.

"Are you having a good rest, Madame Colette? I'm almost invisible, you know. Tomorrow I shan't have quite so much to do: my beef stew is in the cellar and the noodle paste's in a cool place, wrapped up in a cloth. Madame Ruby, you must bring me back twelve cups and saucers; that clumsy fool of a Lucie has brought off a double again. For an idiot, there's no one to touch that girl! Now, *you* . . . have you been at the brandy? No more than one glass, I hope.''

As she spoke, she searched Madame Ruby's face. But the latter kept her head slightly downcast and her gray eyes half closed to avoid the accusing glance. Suddenly the suspicious one gave up and sat down heavily.

"You're just an old soak . . . Oh, my legs!''

"You is needing rest," suggested Madame Ruby.

"Easy enough to say. My best kitchen maid's coming back tomorrow," explained Madame Suzanne. "After tomorrow I'm a lady of leisure.''

She yawned and stretched.

"At this time of night, I've no thought beyond my bath and my bed. Madame Ruby, will you try and shut the rabbit in? The parakeets are all behind the screen and covered up. Are you taking Slough in with you? Oh, and then tomorrow morning, while I think of it . . ."

"Yes, yes, yes, yes!" broke in Madame Ruby, almost beside herself. "Go to bed."

"Really, who do you think you're talking to?"

Madame Suzanne wished us good night with offended dignity. I let the little dog out in the courtyard for a minute while Madame Ruby whistled in vain for Baptiste the rabbit. The night was murmurous and warmer than the day. Three or four lighted windows, the clouded sky patched here and there with stars, the cry of some night bird over this unfamiliar place made my throat tighten with anguish. It was an anguish without depth; a longing to weep which I could master as soon as I felt it rise. I was glad of it because it proved that I could still savor the special taste of loneliness.

———

The next morning, there was a fine drizzle, Under her folded blanket, Pati lay awake and motionless. Her wide-open eyes said, "I know it's raining. There's nothing to hurry for." Through my open window I could feel the dampness, which I find friendly, and I could hear the soft chatter of the parakeets. Their aviary was luxuriously mounted on wheels and had been placed under the shelter of the tiled roof.

Promptly renouncing the idea of "bullying" the workmen who, forty miles away, were digging my soil, painting my wall, and installing my septic tank, I rang for my coffee and slipped on my dressing gown.

Out in the courtyard, Madame Ruby, wearing a mackintosh, gloves, and a little white cap, was loading hampers and empty bottles into her car. She was agile, without an ounce of superfluous flesh. The beautiful, ambiguous rhythm of her movements and the sexless strength which directed them inclined me to excuse her gesture of the night before. Could I have admitted that a man might desire Miss Cooney? Would I have thought it decent for Miss Cooney to fall in love with a man?

The half-bred greyhound took its place beside her. Just as the rough, battered old car was starting up, Monsieur Daste ran up in his dressing gown and gave Madame Ruby his letters to post. When she had gone, he crossed the courtyard cautiously, wrinkling up his nose under the rain. He lost one of his slippers and shook his bare foot in a comic, old-maidish way. Lucie, who had just come in behind my back, saw me laughing.

"Monsieur Daste doesn't like the rain, does he, Lucie?"

"No, he simply can't stand it. Good morning, Madame. When it's raining, he stays indoors. He plays *belote* with those two ladies and he always wins. Will Madame have her breakfast in bed or at the table?"

"I'd rather have it at the table."

She pushed my books and papers to one side and arranged the coffeepot and its satellites. She was very gentle and very concentrated as she slowly and carefully performed these duties. Her skin was smooth and amber-colored, and her eyelashes, like her hair, thick and curling. She seemed to be rather timid. By the side of the big cup she laid a rain-wet rose.

"What a pretty rose! Thank you, Lucie."

"It's not me, it's Madame Ruby."

She blushed fierily, not daring to raise her eyes. I pitied her secretly for being the victim of a disturbance which she must find surprising and vaguely painful.

The flying, almost invisible rain, so much more springlike than yesterday's parched sunshine, beckoned me outdoors. My loyal dog was willing to admit that this fine, powdery rain not only did not wet one but made smells more exciting and was propitious to sneezing.

Under the eaves, Monsieur Daste was taking a chilly little walk. Shivering slightly, he was walking thirty paces to and fro without putting a foot outside the narrow dry strip.

"It's raining!" he shouted at me as if I were deaf.

"But so little . . ."

I stopped close behind him to admire the sheltered parakeets with their tiny, thoughtful foreheads and their wide-set eyes. To my great surprise, they had all fallen silent.

"Are they as frightened of rain as all that?"

"No," said Monsieur Daste. "It's because I'm here. You don't believe me?"

He went closer to the cage. Some of the parakeets flew away and pressed themselves against the bars.

"Whatever have you done to them?"

"Nothing."

He was laughing all over his face and enjoying my astonishment.

"Nothing?"

"Absolutely nothing. That's just what's so interesting."

"Then you must go away."

"Not till it stops raining. Look at that one on the lowest perch."

He slid his manicured forefinger between two bars of the aviary and there was a great fluttering of wings inside.

"Which? There are three all alike."

"Alike to you, perhaps. But not to me. I can pick it out at once. It's the most cowardly one."

One of the parakeets—I think it was the one he was

pointing at—gave a scream. Almost involuntarily, I hit Monsieur Daste on the arm and he stepped back, shaking his hand. He was astonished, but decided to laugh.

"You've only got to leave those parakeets in peace," I said angrily. "Stop tormenting them."

His gaze wandered from the birds to me and back again. I could read nothing in that pleasant neutral face, as far removed from ugliness as it was from beauty, but unresentful surprise and a gaiety that I found extremely ill timed.

"I'm not tormenting them," he protested. "But they know me."

"So does the dog," I thought, seeing Pati's hackles stiffen all along her back. The idea that I might have to spend three weeks in the company of a maniac, possibly an enemy of all animals, profoundly depressed me. At that very moment, Monsieur Daste produced his "huisipisi" for Pati's benefit. She attacked him with all her might and he fled with a comic agility, his hands in his pockets and his shoulders hunched up. I stood perfectly still while she chased him around me. But the chase turned into a game and when Monsieur Daste stopped, out of breath, the dog counted the truce as a victory. She insisted on my congratulating her and looked graciously on her adversary.

During the following days she accepted that irritating "huisipisi" as the signal for a game. But she growled when Monsieur Daste pointed at her or teased her with that tapering, aggressive, minatory forefinger. Comfortably wedged on my forearm with her chest expanded and her eyes bulging, she sniffed the soft dampness with delight.

"She looks like an owl," said Monsieur Daste dreamily.

"Do you frighten owls too?"

To protest his innocence more effectively, Monsieur Daste drew his white, naked hands out of his pockets.

"Good heavens, no, Madame! They interest me . . . certainly they interest me. But . . . I keep away. I must admit I keep well away from them."

He hunched his shoulders up to his ears and scrutinized the sky, where a diffused yellow glow and pale blue patches that promised fine weather were beginning to appear between the clouds. I went off to explore with my dog.

The well-being that rewards me when I exchange my town flat for a hotel does not last very long. Not only do the obligation to work and my usual everyday worries soon take the edge off it but I know all too well the dangers of hotel life. Unless that drifting, irresponsible existence is either completely carefree or organized according to a strict timetable, it always tends to become demoralizing. The main reason for this is that people who really mean nothing to us acquire an artificial importance. At Bella-Vista I had no choice except between the seclusion of a convalescent and the sociability of a passenger on a liner. Naturally, I chose the sociability. I was all the more inclined for it after my first visit to the little house I had bought, I returned from it so disillusioned about landed property that I went and confided my disappointment to Madame Suzanne. I made no secret of the fact that I would be only too glad to sell my bit of land again. She listened earnestly and asked me detailed questions.

"How many square yards did you say you had?"

"Square yards? It comes to five acres. Very nearly."

"But come, that's quite a decent size! What's wrong with it, then?"

"Oh, everything! You should see the state it's in!"

"How many rooms?"

"Five, if you count the kitchen."

"Count it. It sounds more impressive. And you've got the sea?"

"It's practically *in* it."

She pushed away her account book and rubbed her polished nails on her palm.

In your place, I'd . . . . But I'm not in your place."

"Do say what you were going to say, Madame Suzanne."

"*I* should see it as a place where people could stop

off. An exclusive little snack bar, a snug little dance floor under the pines. With your name, why, my dear, it's a gold mine!"

"Madame Suzanne, it's not gold I'm wanting. What I want is a little house and some peace."

"You're talking like a child. As if one could have any peace without money! I know what I'm talking about. So it's not getting on as fast as you think it should, your cottage?"

"I can't quite make out. The builders play bowls in the alley under the trees. And they've made a charming little camping ground by the well. Open-air fire, fish soup . . . grilled sausages, bottles of *vin rosé* too: they offered me a glass."

Madame Suzanne was so amused that she flung herself back in her chair and slapped her thighs.

"Madame Ruby! Come and listen to this!"

Her partner came over to us, with a napkin over one hand and the middle finger of the other capped with a thimble. For the first time, I saw her occupied in a thoroughly feminine way and wearing round spectacles with transparent frames. She went on gravely embroidering drawn threadwork while Madame Suzanne went over "the misfortunes of Madame Colette."

"You look like a boy sewing, Madame Ruby!"

As if offended, Madame Suzanne took the napkin from her friend's hands and held it under my nose.

"It's true that embroidering suits her about as well as sticking a feather in her behind. But look at the work itself! Isn't it exquisite?"

I admired the tiny regular lattices and Madame Suzanne ordered tea for the three of us. An intermittent mistral was blowing. It would be silent for some moments, then give a great shriek and send columns of white sand whirling across the courtyard, half burying the anemones and the pansies. Then it would crouch behind the wall, waiting to spring again.

During this first week, I had not enjoyed one entire warm spring day. We had not had one single day of that real spring weather which soothes one's body and blessedly relaxes one's brain. The departure of the two boys, followed by that of the lady in black and her withered daughter, gave the partners plenty of free time. My only idea was to get away, yet, against my will, I was growing used to the place. That mysterious attraction of what we do not like is always dangerous. It is fatally easy to go on staying in a place which has no soul, provided that every morning offers us the chance to escape.

I knew the timetable of the buses which passed along the main road, three miles away, and which would have put me down at a station. But my daily mail quenched my thirst for Paris. Every afternoon at teatime, I left my work, which was sticking badly, and joined "those women" in a little room off the drawing room which they called their boudoir. I would hear the light step of Monsieur Daste on the wooden staircase as he came down eager for tea and one of his favorite delicacies. This consisted of two deliciously light pieces of flaky pastry sandwiched together with cheese or jam and served piping hot. After dinner I made a fourth at poker or *belote* and reproached myself for doing so. There is always something suspect about things which are as easy as all that.

My griffon bitch, at least, was happy. She was enjoying all the pleasures of a concierge's dog. In the evenings, she left her nest in the woolen hood to sit on Madame Ruby's lap. She noted and listed these new patterns of behavior, keeping her ears open for gossip and her nose alert for smells. She continued to react against Monsieur Daste, but as a wary, intelligent dog rather than as his born enemy.

"Madame Suzanne, what does one do in this part of the world to make workmen get on with the job?"

She shrugged her shoulders. "Offer them a bonus. I know *I* wouldn't offer one."

"Isn't you better give your camping builders a kick in the pants?" suggested Madame Ruby.

She jabbed the air with her needle.

"Tsk, tsk!" said Madame Suzanne reprovingly. "Pour us out some tea and don't be naughty. Drink it hot, Madame Colette. I heard you coughing again this morning when I was getting up at six."

"Did I make as much noise as all that?"

"No, but we're next door. And your hanging cupboard is in a recess so that it juts out right at the back of our . . ."

She stopped short and blushed as violently as an awkward child.

"Our apartment," Madame Ruby suggested lamely.

"That's right. Our apartment."

She put down her cup and threw her arm around Madame Ruby's shoulders with an indescribable look —a look from which all constraint had vanished.

"Don't worry, my poor old darling. When you've said a thing, you've said it. Ten years of friendship —that's nothing to be ashamed of. It's a long-term agreement."

The tweed-jacketed embroidress gave her an understanding glance over her spectacles.

"Of course, I wouldn't talk of such things in front of old Daddy Daste . . . He'll be back soon, won't he?"

"He wasn't at lunch today," I observed.

I was promptly ashamed of having noticed his absence. Petty observations, petty kindnesses, petty pieces of spite—indications, all of them, that my awareness was becoming sharper, yet deteriorating too. One begins by noticing the absence of a Monsieur Daste and soon one descends to "The lady at table 6 took three helpings of French beans . . ." Horrors, petty horrors.

"No," said Madame Suzanne. "He went off early to fetch his car from Nice."

"I didn't know Monsieur Daste had a car."

"Good gracious, yes," said Madame Ruby. "He came here by car and by accident. The car in the ditch and Daddy Daste slightly stunned, with a nest beside him."

"Yes, a nest. I expect the shock is made the nest fall off a tree."

"Wasn't it a scream?" said Madame Suzanne. "A nest! Can't you just see it!"

"Do you like Monsieur Daste, Madame Suzanne?"

She half closed her blue eyes and blew smoke from her painted mouth and her nostrils.

"I like him very much in one way. He's a good client. Tidy, pleasant, and all that. But in another way, I can't stand him. Yet I've not a word to say against him."

"A nest . . ." I said again.

"Ah, that strikes you, doesn't it? There were even three young ones lying dead around the nest."

"Young ones? What kind of bird?"

She shrugged her plump shoulders.

"I haven't any idea. He got off with some bruises and he's been here ever since. It's fifteen days now, isn't it, Ruby?"

"Two weeks," answered Madame Ruby managerially. "He paid his second the day before yesterday."

"And what's Monsieur Daste's job in life?"

Neither of the two friends answered immediately and their silence forced me to notice their uncertainty.

"Well," said Madame Suzanne. "He's the head of a department in the Ministry of the Interior."

She leaned forward with her elbows on her knees and her eyes fastened on mine as if she expected me to protest.

"Does that seem very unlikely, Madame Suzanne?"

"No! Oh, no! But I did not know that civil servants were usually so good at climbing. You should just see how that man can climb. *Really* climb."

The two friends turned simultaneously toward the window, which was darkening to blue as the night came in.

"What do you mean, really climb?"

"Up a tree," said Madame Ruby. "We is not seen him go up, we is seen him coming down. Backward, a tiny step at a time, like this."

With her hands she mimed an acrobatic descent down a mast on a knotted rope.

"A tall tree in the wood, over toward the sea. One evening before you arrived. One of those days when it was so hot, so lovely you is no idea."

"No," I said sarcastically. "I certainly haven't any idea. For over a week I've been disgusted with your weather. I suppose Monsieur Daste was trying to dazzle you with his agility?"

"Just imagine!" cried Madame Suzanne. "He didn't even see us. We were under the tamarisks."

She blushed again. I liked that violent way she had of blushing.

"Madame Suzanne," said Madame Ruby phlegmatically, "you is telling your story all upside down."

"No, I'm not! Madame Colette will understand me, all right! We were sitting side by side and I had my arm around Ruby, like that. We felt rather close to each other, both in the same mood and not spied on all the time as we are in this hole."

She cast a furious glance in the direction of the kitchen.

"After all, it's worth something, a good moment like that! There's no need to talk or to kiss each other like schoolgirls. Is what I'm saying so very absurd?"

She gave her companion a look which was a sudden affirmation of loyal love. I answered no with a movement of my head.

"Well, there we were," she went on. "Then I heard a noise in a tree, too much noise for it to be a cat. I was frightened. I'm brave, really, you know, but I always start by being frightened. Ruby made a sign to me not to move, so I don't move. Then I hear someone's shoe soles scraping and then *poof!* from the ground. And then we see Daddy Daste rubbing his hands and dusting the knees of his trousers and going off up to Bella-Vista. What do you think of that?''

"Funny," I said mechanically.

"Very funny indeed, I think," she said. But she did not laugh.

She poured herself a second cup of tea and lit another cigarette. Madame Ruby, sitting very upright, went on embroidering with agile fingers. For the first time, I noticed that, away from their usual occupations, the two friends did not seem happy or even peaceful. Without going back on the instant liking I had felt for the American, I was beginning to think that Madame Suzanne was the more interesting and more worth studying of the two. I was struck, not only by her fierce, indiscreet jealousy which flared up on the least provocation, but by a kind of protective vigilance, by the way she made herself a buffer between Ruby and all risks, between Ruby and all worries. She gave her all the easy jobs which a subordinate could have done, sending her to the station or to the shops. With perfect physical dignity, Madame Ruby drove the car, unloaded the hampers of eggs and vegetables, cut the roses, cleaned out the parakeets' cage, and offered her lighter to the guests. Then she would cross her sinewy legs in their thick woolen stockings and bury herself in an English or American magazine. Madame Suzanne did not read. Occasionally she would pick up a local paper from a table, saying: "Let's have a look at the *Messenger*," and, five minutes later, drop it again. I was beginning to appreciate her modes of relaxing, so typical of an illiterate woman. She had such an active, intelligent way of doing nothing, of looking about her, of letting her cigarette go out. A really idle person never lets a cigarette go out.

Madame Ruby also dealt with the letters and, when necessary, typed in three languages. But Madame Suzanne said that she "inspired" them and Madame Ruby, nodding her beautiful faded chestnut head, agreed. Teatime cleared Madame Suzanne's head and she would communicate her decisions in my presence. Whether from trustfulness or vanity, she did not mind thus letting me know that her eccentric summer clients did not mind what they paid and demanded privacy even more than comfort. They planned their stays at Bella-Vista a long time ahead.

"Madame Ruby," said Madame Suzanne suddenly, as if in response to a sudden outburst of the mistral, "I hope to goodness you haven't shut the gate onto the road? Otherwise Daddy Daste won't see it and he'll crash into it with his car."

"I asked Paulius to light the little arc lamp at half past six."

"Good. Now, Madame Ruby, we'll have to think about answering those two August clients of ours. They want their usual two rooms. But do remember the Princess and her masseur also want rooms in August. Our two Boche hussies, and the Princess, and Fernande and her gigolo—that's a whole set that's not on speaking terms. But they know each other . . . they've known each other for ages . . . and they can't stand one another. So, Madame Ruby, first of all you're to write to the Princess.

She explained at considerable length, knitting her penciled eyebrows. She addressed Ruby as "Madame" and used the intimate "*tu*" with a bourgeois, marital ceremoniousness. As she spoke, she kept looking at her friend just as an anxious nurse might scrutinize the complicated little ears, the eyelids, and the nostrils of an immensely well-looked-after child. She would smooth down a silvery lock on her forehead, straighten her tie, flatten her collar, or pick a stray white thread off her jacket.

The expression on her face—it was tired and making no attempt just then to hide its tiredness—seemed to me very far from any "perverted" fussing. I use the word "perverted" in its usual modern sense. She saw that I was watching her and gave me a frank, warm smile which softened the blue eyes that often looked so hard.

"It's no news to you," she said, "that our clientele's rather special. After all, it was Grenigue who gave you our address. At Christmas and Easter, you won't find a soul. But come back in July and you'll have any amount of copy. You realize that, with only ten rooms in all, we have to put up prices a bit; our real season only lasts three months. I'll tell you something that'll make you laugh. Last summer, what do you think arrived? A little old couple, husband and wife, at least a hundred and sixty between them. Two tiny little things with an old manservant crumbling to bits, who asked if they could inspect the rooms, as if we were a palace! I said to them—as nicely as possible—'There's some mistake. You see this is a rather special kind of inn.' They didn't want to go. But I insisted, I tried to find words to make myself understood, old-fashioned words, you know. I said, 'It's a bit naughty-naughty, so to speak. People come here and sow their wild oats, as it were. You can't stay here.' Do you know what she answered, that little old grandmother? 'And who told you, Madame, that we don't want to sow some wild oats too?' They went away, of course. But she had me there, all right! Madame Ruby, do you know what the time is? Time you gave that embroidery a rest. I can't hear a sound in the dining room and the courtyard's not lit up. Whatever's the staff thinking about?''

"I'll go and ask Lucie," said Madame Ruby, promptly getting to her feet.

"No," shouted Madame Suzanne. "I must go and see to the dinner. You don't suppose the leg of mutton's anxiously waiting for *you*, do you?''

She was trembling with sudden rage. Her lips were quivering with desire to burst out into a furious tirade. To stop herself, she made a rush to the door. As she did so, there was the sound of a motor engine and the headlights of a car swept the courtyard.

"Daddy Daste," announced Madame Suzanne.

"Why isn't that man switched off his headlights to come in? He might at least do that."

Pati, suddenly woken up, flung herself at the french window, from etiquette rather than from hostility. The dry breath of the mistral entered along with Monsieur Daste. He was rubbing his hands, and his impersonal face at last bore an individual accent. This was a small newly-made wound, triangular in shape, under his right eye.

"Hello, Monsieur Daste! You is wounded? Pebble? A branch? An attack? Is the car damaged?"

"Good evening, ladies," said Monsieur Daste politely. "No, no, nothing wrong with the car. She's going splendidly. This," he put his hand to his cheek, "isn't worth bothering about."

"All the same, I'm going to give you some peroxide," said Madame Suzanne, who had come up to him and was examining the deeply incised little wound at close range. "Don't cover it up, then it'll dry quicker. A nail? A bit of flying flint?"

"No," said Monsieur Daste. "Just a . . . bird."

"What, *another* one?" said Madame Ruby.

Madame Suzanne turned to her friend with a reproving look.

"What do you mean, another one? There's nothing so very astonishing about it."

"Quite so. Nothing so very astonishing," agreed Monsieur Daste.

"It's full of night birds around here."

"Full," said Monsieur Daste.

"The headlights dazzle them and they dash themselves against the windshield."

"Exactly," concluded Monsieur Daste. "I'm delighted to be back at the Bella-Vista again. That Corniche road at night! To think that there are people who actually drive on it for pleasure! I shall do justice to the dinner, Madame Suzanne!"

Nevertheless we noticed at dinner that Monsieur Daste ate nothing but the sweet. I noticed this mainly because Madame Ruby kept up a stream of encouragement from her table.

"Hello, Monsieur Daste! Is good for you to keep your strength up!"

"But I assure you I don't feel in the least weak," Monsieur Daste kept politely assuring her.

In fact, his abstinence had endowed him with the bright flush of satiety. He was drinking water with a slightly inebriated expression.

Madame Ruby raised her large hand sententiously.

"Leg of mutton *Bretonne* is very good against birds, Monsieur Daste!"

I remember it was that evening that we played our first game of poker. My three partners loved cards. In order to play better, they retired into the depths of themselves, leaving their faces unconsciously exposed. Studying them amused me more than the game. In any case, I play poker extremely badly and was scolded more than once. I was amused to note that Monsieur Daste only "opened" when forced to and then only with obvious reluctance, but good cards gave him spasms of nervous yawns which he managed to suppress by expanding his nostrils. His little wound had been washed and around it a bruised area was already turning purple, showing how violent the impact had been.

Madame Ruby played a tough game, compressing her full lips, and asking for cards and raising the bid by signs. I was astonished to see her handling the cards with agile but brutal fingers, using a thumb which was much thicker than I had realized. As to Madame Suzanne, she seemed set in her tracks like a bloodhound. She showed not the slightest emotion, pulled each card out slowly before declaring with an air of detachment: "Good for me!"

The smoke accumulated in horizontal layers and between two rounds I reproached myself for the inertia which kept me sitting there. "Perhaps I'm still not quite well," I told myself with a kind of hopefulness.

Suddenly the mistral stopped blowing and the silence fell on us so brutally that it awakened the sleeping griffon. She emerged from her knitted hood and asked clearly, with her eyes and her pricked ears, what time it was.

"Huisipisi, huisipisi!" said Monsieur Daste maliciously.

She stared at him, sniffed the air about his person, and put her two front paws on the table. From there, by stretching her thick little neck, she could just reach Monsieur Daste's hands.

"How she loves me!" said Monsieur Daste. "Huisipisi . . ."

The dog seemed to be searching for a particular spot and to find it just under the edge of Monsieur Daste's cuff. She smelled it with her knowing black nostrils, then she tasted it with her tongue.

"She's tickling me! Madame Suzanne, you pray too long to the goddess of luck while you're shuffling the cards. On with the game!"

"Monsieur Daste, why do you always say 'huisipisi' to my dog? Is it a magic password?"

He fluttered his little hands about his face.

"The breeze," he said. "The wind in the fir trees. Wings . . . Huisipisi . . . Things that fly . . . Even things that skim over the ground in a very . . . very *silky* way. Rats."

"Boo!" cried Madame Suzanne. "I've a horror of mice. So, imagine, a *rat*! On with the game yourself,

Monsieur Daste. Madame Colette, don't forget the kitty. I believe you're thinking more about your next novel than our little poker game.''

In this she was wrong. Alone in this equivocal guest house, during the pause before the harvest of its summer debauch, I was aware of a complex and familiar mental state. In that state a peculiar pleasure blunts the sharp edge of my longing for my friends, my home, and my real life. Yet is there anyone who is not deluded about the setting of their "real" life? Was I not breathing here and now, among these three strangers, what I call the very oxygen of travel? My thoughts could wander as lazily as they pleased; I was free of any burden of love; I was immersed in that holiday emptiness in which morning brings a light-hearted intoxication and evening a compulsion to waste one's time and to suffer. Everything you love strips you of part of yourself: the Madame Suzannes rob you of nothing. Answering the few careless questions they ask takes nothing out of you. "How many pages do you do a day? All those letters you get every day and all those ones you write, don't you have to cudgel your brains over them? You don't happen to know an authoress who lives all the year round at Nice—a tall woman with pince-nez?" The Madame Suzannes don't catechize you; they tell you about themselves. Sometimes, of course, they keep aggressively silent about some great secret which is always

rising to their lips and being stifled. But a secret is
exacting and deafens us with its clamor.

In many ways, I found Bella-Vista satisfying. It
revived old habits from my solitary days: the itch for
the arrival of the postman, my curiosity about pass-
ers-by who leave no permanent trace. I felt sympathetic toward the discredited pair of friends. At Bella-
Vista I ate admirably and worked atrociously. More-
over, I was putting on weight there.

"Four last rounds," announced Madame Suzanne.
"Monsieur Daste, you open for the last time. After-
ward, I'll stand you a bottle of champagne. I think
that ought to wake Madame Ruby up. There hasn't
been a sound from her all the evening."

Her blue eyes shot a glance of fierce reproach at
her impassive friend.

"You is usually hear me play poker at the top of
my voice?"

Madame Suzanne did not answer and, as soon as
the last round was over, went off to get the champagne. While she was going down to the cellar, Madame Ruby stood up, stretched her arms and her firm
shoulders till the joints cracked. Then she opened the
door between the dining room and the boudoir, listened in the direction of the kitchen, and came back
again. She seemed absentminded, preoccupied by
some care which made her full mouth look ugly and
dulled the large gray eyes under the eyebrows which

were paler than her forehead. That evening, the ambiguity of all her features, always disturbing, seemed almost repellent. She was biting the inside of her cheek but forced herself to stop gnawing it when her friend returned, out of breath, with a bottle of *brut* under each arm.

"This is really old," announced Madame Suzanne. "Some remains of the '06. You don't think I pour *that* down the gullets of the summer visitors. It's not iced but the cellar's cool. I don't know if you agree with me that it's nice to have a wine now and then that doesn't make a block of ice in your stomach. Madame Ruby, where are there some pliers? These bottles are wired in the old-fashioned way."

"I'll call Lucie," suggested the American.

Madame Suzanne looked at her almost furiously.

"For God's sake, can't you give Lucie a little peace? For one thing, she's gone to bed. For another, you'll certainly find some sort of pliers in the office."

We drank each other's health. Madame Ruby magically gulped down a large glass in one swallow, throwing her head back in a way which proved how much drinking was a habit with her. Madame Suzanne mimicked the toasts with which drinkers in the Midi raise their glasses: "To your very good!" "Much appreciated! Likewise!" Monsieur Daste closed his eyes like a cat afraid of splashing itself when it laps. Sitting opposite me in the depths of one of the English armchairs, he drank the perfect old champagne, whose bubbles gave out a faint scent of roses as they burst, in tiny sips. The bruise which was now clearly visible around the little triangular wound on his cheek made him seem, for some reason, likable, less definitely human. I like a fox terrier to have a round spot by its eye and a tortoiseshell cat to show an orange crescent or a black patch on its temple. A large mole or freckle on our cheek, a neat well-placed scar, one eye that is slightly larger than the other: all such things mark us out from the general human anonymity.

Madame Suzanne inclined the neck of the second bottle over our goblets and drew our attention to the mushroom-shaped cork, which had acquired the texture of hard wood with age.

"Two bottles among four of us. Quite an orgy! But we'll see better than that in this house this summer."

"We can see it here and now, if you like," said Madame Ruby promptly, pushing her empty glass toward the bottle.

Madame Suzanne gave her friend a warning look.

"Moderation in all things, Madame Ruby. Would you be an angel and go and find that fool of a Slough? And shut the rabbit up, if you can! Have you covered up the parakeets?"

Through the light buzzing of the wine in my ears, I listened to those ritual phrases, not unlike "count-ing-out rhymes." I know by experience how their sound, their fatal recurrence can be like longed-for dew or a faint, neutral blessing. I know, too, that they can also fall like a branding iron on a place already seared.

But that night I was all benevolence. Pati, who was also getting fatter at Bella-Vista, waddled peacefully into the courtyard and I listened gratefully to Madame Ruby's voice outside announcing that it was going to be fine.

As I stood up, my spectacles and my room key slipped off my knees. As they fell, Monsieur Daste's hand reached out and caught them with such a swift, perfectly timed movement that I hardly had time to see his gesture. "Ah," I thought. "So he's not quite human, this climber."

We all separated without further words like people who have the sense not to prolong the pleasures of a superficial gaiety and cordiality to the point of imprudence. Still under the spell of my optimism, I complimented Monsieur Daste on the appearance of his little wound. I did not tell him that it brought out the character, at once intelligent and uninteresting, of his face. He seemed enchanted. He bridled and passed one hand coquettishly over his ear to smooth his hair.

—

Lucie did not have to wake me the next morning. When she came in with the tray and the rose, I was already dressed and standing at my open french window, contemplating the fine weather.

Thirteen years ago, I did not know what spring or summer in the Midi could be. I knew nothing of that irruption, that victorious invasion of a season of serenity, of that enduring pact between warmth, color, and scent. That morning I took to longing for the sea salt on my hands and lips and to thinking of my patch of land where my picnicking workmen were drinking *vin rosé* and eating salami.

"Lucie, what beautiful weather!"

"The proper weather for the season. About time too. It's kept us waiting long enough."

As she arranged my breakfast and the daily rose on the table, the dark-haired maid answered me absently. I looked at her and saw that she was pale. Her pallor and a certain troubled look made her more attractive. She had put a little rouge on her beautiful mouth.

"Hello, Madame Colette!"

I answered Madame Ruby, who, dressed all in blue, with a narrow tight-fitting shirt and a beret pulled over one ear, was loading up her hampers.

My dog rushed at her, gave her her military salute, and danced around her.

"You is not want to come with me?"

"I'd love to."

"While I do my shopping, you gives good advice to your pioneers."

"Excellent idea!"

"You say the mason: 'Dear friend.' You say the man who does the roof: 'My boy.' You say the little painter: 'Where is you get made the smart white blouse what suits you so well?' You turn on the charm! Perhaps that works."

"Ah, you know how to talk to men, Madame Ruby! Hold Pati. Just let me get a pullover and I'll be with you."

I went into the bathroom for a moment. When I returned, Lucie and Madame Ruby, one standing perfectly still in my room and the other stationed in the courtyard, were looking at each other across the intervening space. The maid did not turn away quickly enough to conceal from me that her eyes were full of fear, gentleness, and tears.

Madame Ruby drove us, fast and well, through the sparse forest, still russet from the annual fires. Between two tracts of pineland were carefully cultivated allotments now green with young beans and marrows, and fenced-off tracts of wild quince with great pink flowers. The much-prized garlic and onion lifted their spears from the light, powdery earth and the growing vines were stretching out their first tendrils. The blue air was now chill but kindly, now full of new and subtle warmth. The blue air of the Estérels rushed to meet us, and moistened the dog's nose. Along the lane which ran into the main road, I could put out my hand as we drove and touch the leaves of the almond trees and the fruit already set and downy.

"The spring is born tonight," said Madame Ruby softly.

Up till then, we had only exchanged a few commonplaces and these last words, spoken in such a low, troubled voice that they were almost inaudible, came as a surprise. They did not demand an answer and I made none. My strange companion sat impassive at the wheel, her chin high and her little beret over one eye. I threw a glance at her firm profile, so unlike a Frenchwoman's, and noted again the coarse ruddy texture of her skin. The back of her neck, emerging from her pullover, looked as strong as a coal heaver's. With a terrible blast of her horn, she swept the sprawling, dusty dogs off the road, to Pati's intense delight, and kept up a stream of blasphemy in English against the heedless cart drivers. "The spring is born tonight." Imprisoned behind the same ambiguous exterior, a brazen, angular female and a collegian in love with a servant girl were both claiming the right to live and to love. Very likely each hated the other.

It seemed a long time before we came to the coast and drove along the edge of the sea where a few bathers were shrieking with cold as they splashed about. We passed through sham villages; pink, silent, and empty, idly blossoming with no one to admire.

At last Madame Ruby put me down in front of my future dwelling. She gave a whistle of ironic commiseration and refused to get out of the car. Raising her forefinger to the level of her pale, bushy eyebrow, she said: "I come and fetch you in three-quarters of an hour. You thinks it is enough for your whole house to be finished?"

She indicated the rampart of hollow bricks, the crater of slaked lime, and the mound of sifted sand which defended my gates, and left me to my fate.

But when she returned, I no longer wanted to leave the place. Instead of the workmen, who were missing one and all, I had found white arum lilies, red roses, a hundred little tulips with pointed cups, purple irises, and pittosporums whose scent paralyzes the will. Leaning over the edge of the well, I had listened to the musical noise of drops that filtered through the broken bricks falling into the water below, while Pati rested after her first encounter with a hedgehog. The interior of the house bore not the slightest resemblance to anything which had charmed me about it at first. But in the little pine wood, the bright drops of liquid resin were guttering in the wind, those drops that congeal almost as soon as they are formed, and tarnish before they fall to the ground. I had treated the mimosa, which flowers all the year round, with scant respect. Feeling like a rich person, I flung my bundle of flowers into the car, on top of the hampers of early artichokes, broad beans, and French beans with which the back seat was loaded.

"Not a soul?" asked Madame Ruby.

"Not a soul! Such luck! It was delightful."

"We used to say that at Bella-Vista too, in the beginning. 'Such luck! Not a soul!' And now . . ."

She raised that clerical chin of hers and started up the car.

"And now we is a little blasé. A little old, both of us."

"It's very beautiful, a friendship that grows old gracefully. Don't you agree?"

"Nobody loves what is old," she said harshly. "Everyone loves what is beautiful, what is young—dangerous. Everyone loves the spring."

On the way back, she did not speak again except to the dog. In any case, I should have been incapable of listening intelligently. I was conscious only of the noonday sun drugging me with light well-being and overwhelming drowsiness. I sat with my eyes closed, aware only of the resonance of a voice which, though nasal, was never shrill and whose deep pitch was as pleasant as the lowest notes of a clarinet. Madame Ruby drove fast, pointing out objects of vituperation to Pati, such as small donkeys, chickens, and other dogs. The griffon responded enthusiastically to all these suggestions, even though they were expressed in English spoken with an American twang.

"O.K.," approved Madame Ruby. "Good for you to learn English. Holiday task. Look to the left, enormous, enormous goose! Wah!"

"Wah!" repeated the little dog, standing up, quite beside herself with excitement, with her front paws against the windshield.

———

Of the few days that followed, I remember only the glorious weather. The weather spread an indulgent blue and gold and purple haze over my work and my worries, over the letters which arrived from Paris, over the full-blown idleness of the workmen, whom I found singing and playing "she loves me, she loves me not" with daisy petals when I revisited my little house. Fine weather, day and night, induced in me an Oriental rebelliousness against the accustomed hours of sleep. I was wide awake at midnight and overwhelmed with the imperative need of a siesta in the afternoon. Laziness, like work, demands to be comfortably organized. Mine sleeps during the day, muses at night, wakes at dawn, and closes the shutters against the unsympathetic light of the hours after lunch. On dark nights and under the first quarter of a slender, rosy moon, the nightingales all burst out together, for there is never a first nightingale.

On this subject, Monsieur Daste made various poetic remarks which did not affect me in the least. For I never bothered less about Monsieur Daste than I did during that week of fine weather. I saw hardly anything even of my hostesses. Their importance faded under the dazzling impact of the season. I did however observe a little poker incident between Madame Ruby and Monsieur Daste one evening. It was a very brief incident, mimed rather than spoken, and in the course of it I had a vision of Madame Ruby flushing the color of copper and clutching the edge of the green table with both hands. At that, Monsieur Daste gathered himself together in a most peculiar way. He seemed to shrink till he became very small and very compact, and as he thrust his lowered brow forward, he gave the impression of drawing back his shoulders behind his head. It was an attitude that blended ill with his prim face and that hair which was neither old nor young. Madame Suzanne promptly laid her hand on her friend's well-groomed head.

"Now, now, my pet! Now, now . . ." she said without raising her voice.

With one accord, the two adversaries resumed a friendly tone and the game went on. As I was not interested in the cause of their quarrel, I made no inquiries. Perhaps Monsieur Daste had cheated. Or perhaps Madame Ruby. Or possibly both of them. I only thought to myself that, had it come to a fight, I should not have backed Monsieur Daste to win.

It was that night, if I am not mistaken, that I was

awakened by a great tumult among the parakeets. As it was silenced almost at once, I did not get up. The next morning, very early, I saw Madame Ruby, trim as usual in white and blue, her rose in her lapel, standing near the aviary. Her back was turned to me and she was attentively studying some object she was holding in her cupped hand. Then she slipped whatever it was into her pocket. I pulled on a dressing gown and opened my french window.

"Madame Ruby, did you hear the parakeets in the night?"

She smiled at me, nodded from the distance, and came up the little steps to shake hands with me.

"Slept well?"

"Not badly. But did you hear, about two in the morning . . ."

She drew out of her pocket a dead parakeet. It was soft and the eye showed bluish between two borders of gray skin.

"What! They're capable of killing each other?"

"So we must suppose," said Madame Ruby, without looking up. "Poor little bird!"

She blew on the cold feathers which parted about a torn, bloodless wound. The dog wanted to be in on the affair and sniffed the bird with that mixture of bewilderment and eroticism which the sight and smell of death so often excites in the living.

"Not so keen, not so keen, little yellow dog. You

begins smell, smell and then you eats. And then ever after, you eats.''

She went off with the bird in her pocket. Then she changed her mind and came back.

"Please, it's better to say nothing to Madame Suzanne. Nor Monsieur Daste. Madame Suzanne is super . . . superstitious. And Monsieur Daste is . . .''

Her prominent eyes, gray as agates, sought mine.

"He is . . . sensitive. It's better to say nothing.''

"I agree.''

She gave me that little salute with her forefinger and I did not see her again till luncheon.

In addition to its usual guests, Bella-Vista was receiving a family from Lausanne: three couples of hiking campers. Their rucksacks, their little tents and battery of aluminum cooking utensils, their red faces and bare knees seemed like the emblems of some inoffensive faith.

Lucie went to and fro between the tables, carrying the chervil omelette, the brains fried in batter, and the ragoût of beef. Her face was thickly powdered and she was languid and absentminded.

Their meal over, the campers spread out a map. With managerial discretion, Madame Suzanne signed to us to come and take our coffee in the "boudoir.'' There was an expression of faint repugnance on her heated face. She gave off her strong perfume which blended ill with that of the ragoût, and she cooled the fire of her complexion with the help of a vast powder puff which never left the pocket of her white blouse.

"Pooh!" she sighed as she fell into a chair. "My goodness, how they fell on the stew, those Switzers! You'll eat God knows what tonight: I haven't a thing left. Those people give me the creeps. So I'm going to treat myself to a little cigar. Where are they off to already, Madame Ruby?"

With a thrust of her chin, Madame Ruby indicated the direction of the sea.

"Over there. Somewhere that isn't got a name, provided it's at least thirty miles away."

"And they sleep on the hard ground. And they drink nothing but water. And it's for idiots like that that our wonderful age invented the railway and the motorcar and the *airplane*! I ask you! As for me sleeping on the ground, the mere idea of ants . . ."

She bit off the end of her little Havana and rolled it carefully between her fingers. Madame Ruby never smoked anything but cigarettes.

"Come, come!" said Monsieur Daste. "Don't speak ill of camping. You must be used to many forms of camping, Madame Ruby? And I'm sure you look much more chic in plus-fours and a woolen shirt and hobnailed shoes than those three Swiss females. Come along now, admit it."

She threw him an ironic glance and displayed her large teeth.

"All right, I admit it," she said. "What about you, Monsieur Daste? Camping? Nights under the open stars? Dangerous encounters? You is a slyboots, Monsieur Daste! Don't deny it!"

Monsieur Daste was flattered. He lowered his chin till it touched his tie, passed his hand over his ear to smooth the hair on his temple, and coquettishly swallowed a mouthful of brandy, which went the wrong way. He was convulsed with choking coughs and only regained his breath under the kindly hammering of Madame Suzanne's hand on his shoulder blades. I must record that, with his face flushed and his streaming eyes bloodshot, Monsieur Daste was unrecognizable.

"Thank you," he said when he could breathe again. "You've saved my life, Madame Suzanne. I can't imagine what could have got stuck in my throat."

"A feather, perhaps," said Madame Ruby.

Monsieur Daste turned his head toward her with an almost imperceptible movement and then became stock-still. Madame Suzanne, who was sucking her cigar, became agitated and said shrilly: "A feather? Whatever will she think of next? A *feather*! You're not ill, are you, Ruby? Now *me*," she went on hurriedly, "you'd never believe what *I* swallowed when I was a kid. A watch spring! But a *huge* watch spring, a positive metal snake, my dears, as long as *that*!

I've swallowed a lot of other things since those days, bigger ones too, if you count insults.''

She laughed, not only with her mouth but with her eyes, and gave a great yawn.

"My children, I doubt very much whether you'll see me again before five o'clock. Madame Ruby, will you look after the Swissies? They're taking sandwiches with them tonight so that they can have dinner on a nice cool carpet of pine needles which'll stick into their behinds.''

"Right,'' said Madame Ruby. "Lucie is made the sandwiches?''

"No, Marguerite. Go and make sure she packs them in greaseproof paper. I've put it all down on their bill.''

Suddenly she extinguished the laugh in her blue eyes and scanned her friend's face closely. "I've sent Lucie to her room. She's not feeling well.''

Having said that, she left the room, jerking her shoulders as she did so. The back of her neck suggested a proud determination which I was the only one to notice. Monsieur Daste, shrunken and tense, had still not moved. Madame Ruby paid not the slightest attention either to Monsieur Daste or to myself before she, too, went out.

———

It was from that moment that I realized I was no longer enjoying myself at Bella-Vista. The saffron

walls and the blue shutters, the Basque roof, the plastered Norman beams, and the Provençal tiles all suddenly seemed to me false and pretentious. A certain
troubled atmosphere and the menace and hostility it
breeds can only interest me if I am personally in-
volved in it. It was not that I repented of feeling
a rather pendulum-like sympathy with my hostesses
which inclined now to Suzanne, now to Ruby. But,
selfishly, I would have preferred them happy, serene
in their old, faithful, reprehensible love that should
have been spiced only with childish quarrels. The fact
remained that I did not see them happy. And as to
faithfulness, the yielding gentleness of a dark-haired
servant girl gave me matter for thought—and disap-
proval.

When I ran into Lucie, when she brought me my
"rose" breakfast about half past seven, I found myself feeling as severe toward Madame Ruby as if she
had been Philemon deceiving Baucis.

I began to suspect "Daddy" Daste, that climber
who had been so ill rewarded for his bird watching. I
began to suspect his mysterious government employ-
ment, his scar adorned with black sticking plaster,
and even what I called his malicious good temper. A
conversation with Madame Ruby might have taught
me more about Monsieur Daste and possibly explained the obvious antipathy he inspired in her. But
Madame Ruby made no attempt to have any private
talk with me.

I remember that, about that very time, the weather changed again. During the twilight of a long April day, the southeast wind began to blow in short gusts, bringing with it a heat which mounted from the soil as from an oven full of burning bread. All four of us were playing bowls. Madame Suzanne kept shaking her white linen sleeves to "air herself" as she sighed: "If it weren't that I want to slim down!"

Bowls is a good game, like all games capable of revealing some trait of character in the expert player. Much to my surprise, Monsieur Daste was "shooter." Before launching his wood, he held it hidden almost behind his back. The arm, the small manicured hand, and the wood rose together and the heavy nailed ball fell on his adversary's with a resounding crack which sent Monsieur Daste into ecstasy.

"On his skull! Bang on top of his skull!" he cried.

Madame Suzanne, the "shooter" of the other side, rated about the same as I did as "marker" for Monsieur Daste's. Sometimes I "mark" very well, sometimes like a complete duffer. Madame Ruby "marked" to perfection, rolling her wood as softly as a ball of wool to within a hairbreadth of the jack. Disdaining our heavy woods, Pati snapped and spat out again innumerable insects which had been driven inland by the approach of a solid wall of purple clouds which was advancing toward us from the sea.

"My children, I can feel the storm coming. The

roots of my hair are hurting me!'' wailed Madame Suzanne.

At the first flash which broke into twigs of incandescent pink as it ran down the sky into the flat sea, Madame Suzanne gave a great ''Ha!'' and covered her eyes.

A warm gust played all around the courtyard, rolling faded flowers, straws, and leaves into wreaths and spirals, and the swallows circled in the air in the same direction. Warm heavy drops splayed on my hands. Madame Ruby ran to the garage, taking great strides, pulled on a black oilskin, and returned to her friend, who had not stirred. White as chalk, her hands over her eyes, the sturdy Suzanne collapsed, weak and tottering, on the shoulder of Madame Ruby, who looked like a dripping lifeboatman.

The strange couple and I ran toward our twin little flights of steps. Having shut Madame Suzanne in her room, Madame Ruby rushed to the rescue of other shipwrecked creatures, such as the bloodthirsty rabbit and the stupid greyhound. She wheeled the aviary into the garage, shouted orders to the two invisible kitchen maids and to Lucie, who stood in a doorway, her loosened hair hanging in a cloud around her pale face. She closed all the banging doors and brought in the cushions from the garden chairs.

From my window, I watched the hurly-burly which the American woman directed with a slightly theatri-

cal calm. Nestled against my arm, my excited dog
followed all that was going on while she waited for
the battle of the elements. She shone in exceptional
circumstances; particularly in great storms which she
boldly defied where a bulldog would have panted with
fear and done his best to die flattened out under an
armchair. A minute dog with a great brain, Pati wel-
comed tempests on land or sea like a joyous stormy
petrel.

Behind me, the violet darkness of the sky, mag-
nificently rent by each flash, was stealing into my
red-and-pink room. Some small, hollow-sounding
thunder which echoed back from the hills decided
to accompany the lightning flashes, and a crushing
curtain of rain, which dropped suddenly from the sky,
made me hastily shut my window.

It was almost time for the real night to close in.
But the passing night of the storm had taken the place
of dusk and I sat down, sullen and unwilling, to my
work. I had begun it without inclination and continued it in a desultory way without being decided
enough to abandon it altogether. The dog, becoming
virtuously quiet as soon as she saw me busy with
papers, gnawed her claws and listened to the thunder
and the rain. I think that both she and I longed with
all our hearts for Paris, for our friends there, for the
reassuring mutter of a city.

The rain, which had fallen from a moderate-sized

cloud which the wind had not had time to shred, stopped suddenly. My ear, made alert by the startling silence, caught the sound of voices on the other side of the partition. I could hear a high voice and a lower one, then the sound of tearful recriminations. "Extraordinary!" I thought. "The fat Madame Suzanne getting herself in such a state because of a storm!"

She did not appear at dinner.

"Madame Suzanne isn't feeling well?" I asked Madame Ruby.

"Her nerves. You is no idea how nervous she is."

"The first storm of the season affects the nerves," said Monsieur Daste, whose opinion no one had asked. "This one is the first . . . but not the last," he added, pointing to wavering flashes on the horizon.

I began to think impatiently of my approaching departure. Bella-Vista could no longer assuage my increasing restlessness and my sense of foreboding. I took my dog out into the courtyard before her usual time. Like a child with new shoes, she deliberately splashed through the puddles of rain which reflected a few stars. I had to scold her to get her away from a frog which she doubtless wanted to bring home and add to her collections in Paris: collections of mammoth bones, ancient biscuits, punctured balls, and sulphur lozenges. Monsieur Daste undermined my authority and egged Pati on with innumerable "huisipisis." The night had stayed warm and its scents made me languid. What tropics exhale more breaths of orange blossom, resin, rain-soaked carnations, and wild peppermint than a spring night in Provence?

After reading in bed, I switched off my lamp rather late and got up to open the door and window so as to let in as much as possible of the meager coolness and the overabundant scent. Standing in the dark room, I remembered that I had not heard Monsieur Daste come in. For the first time, I found something unpleasant in the thought of Monsieur Daste's small, agile feet walking, on a moonless night, not far from my open and accessible window. I know from experience how easily a fixed idea of a terror can take concrete shape and I invariably take pains to crush their first, faint intimations. Various mnemonic tricks and musical rhymes served to lull me into a dream in which printed letters danced before me, and I was asleep when the french window which led into my hostesses' room was clicked open.

I sat up in bed and heard, from the other side, a deep chest inhaling and exhaling the air. In the silence which foreboded other storms, I was also aware of the slither of two bare feet on my neighbors' stone steps.

"You makes me die of heat with your nerves," said Madame Ruby in a muffled voice. "The storm's over."

The rectangle of my open window was suddenly lit

up. I realized that Madame Suzanne had turned on the ceiling light in her room.

"Idiot! I'm naked," whispered Ruby furiously.

The light was promptly switched off.

"Too late. Daste's right opposite, in the courtyard."

I heard a stifled exclamation and the thump of two heavy feet landing on the wooden floor. Madame Suzanne went over to her friend.

"Where d'you say he is?"

"Over by the garage."

"It's quite a long way off."

"Not for him. In any case, it is telling him nothing he doesn't know."

"Oh don't . . . oh, don't."

"Don't get upset, darling. There, there . . ."

"My pet . . . oh, my pet!"

"Shut up so I can listen. He's opening the door of the garage."

They went silent for a long moment. Then Madame Suzanne whispered vehemently: "Get it well into your head that if they separate us, if they come here to . . ."

Madame Ruby's light whistle ordered her to be quiet. The dog had growled and I gently closed my hand over her muzzle.

"Suppose I shoot?" said the voice of Madame Ruby.

"Are you quite mad?"

This startling interchange was followed by a scuffle of bare feet. I imagined that Madame Suzanne was dragging her friend back into the room.

"Really, Richard, you must be mad. Aren't we in a bad enough mess as it is? Isn't it enough for you to have got Lucie in the family way without wanting to put a bullet through Daste into the bargain? You couldn't control yourself just for once, could you? No, of course not. You men are all the same. Come on, now. No more nonsense. Come indoors, and for heaven's sake, stay there."

The french window shut and there was complete silence.

I made no further attempt to sleep. My astonishment was soon over. Had Madame Suzanne's cry of revelation really given me a genuine surprise? What excited my interest and moved me profoundly was the thought of Madame Suzanne's vigilance, the discreet and devoted cynicism she interposed between the disguised, suspected "Madame" Ruby and the malevolent little Daste.

If the idle looker-on in me exclaimed delightedly, "What a story!" my honorable side wanted me to keep the story to myself. I have done so for a very long time.

Toward three in the morning, the wind changed and a fresh storm attacked Bella-Vista. It was accompanied by continuous thunder and slanting rain. In the moment or two it took to gather up my strewn, sopping papers, my nightdress was soaked and clung to my body. The dog followed all my movements, holding herself ready for any contingency. "Have we got to swim? Have we got to run away?" I set her an example of immovable patience and made her a cave out of a scarf. In the shelter of this she played at shipwrecks and desert islands and even at earthquakes.

Now against a background of total darkness, now against a screen lit up with lightning flashes and driving rain. I reconstructed the neighboring couple, the man and the woman. Two normal people, undoubtedly with the police on their track, lay side by side in the next room, awaiting their fate.

Perhaps the woman's head rested on the man's shoulder while they exchanged anxious speculations. In imagination I saw again the back of "Madame" Ruby's neck, that thumb, that roughened cheek, that large, well-shaved upper lip. Then I dwelt again on Madame Suzanne and wished good luck to that heroic woman; so jealous and so protective; so terrified, yet ready to face anything.

Daybreak brought a gray drizzle on the heels of the tornado and sleep overtook me at last. No hand knocked on my door or laid my breakfast tray with its customary rose on my table. The unwonted silence awakened me and I rang for Lucie. It was Marguerite who came.

"Where is Lucie?"

"I don't know, Madame. But won't I do instead?"

Under the impalpable rain, the courtyard and climbing roses torn from their trellis had the aspect of October. "The train, the first train! I won't stay another twenty-four hours!"

In the wide-open garage, I caught sight of the white linen overall and the dyed gold hair of Madame Suzanne and I went out to join her. She was sitting on an upturned pail and candidly let me see her ravaged face. It was the face of an unhappy middle-aged wife, the eyes small and swollen and the cheeks scoured with recent tears.

"Look," she said. "A nice sight, isn't it?"

At her feet lay the nineteen parakeets, dead. Assassinated would be a better word for the frenzy with which they had been destroyed. They had been torn and almost pulped in a peculiarly revolting way. The dog sniffed at the birds from a distance and planted herself at my heels.

"Monsieur Daste's car isn't in the garage any longer?"

Madame Suzanne's little swollen eyes met my own.

"Nor is *he* in the house," she said. "Gone. After doing that, it's hardly surprising."

With her foot, she pushed away a headless parakeet.

"If you're sure he did it, why don't you complain
to the police? In your place, I should certainly lodge
a complaint."

"Yes. But you're not in my place."

She put a hand on my shoulder.

"Ah, my dear, lodge a complaint! You don't know
what you're talking about. Besides," she added,
"he'd paid his bill for the week. He doesn't owe us a
farthing."

"Is he a madman?"

"I'd like to believe so. I must go and find Paulius
and get him to bury all this. Was there something you
wanted?"

"Nothing special. As I told you already, I'm leaving. Tomorrow. Or even today unless that's quite
impossible."

"Just as you like," she said indifferently. "Today,
if you'd rather. Because tomorrow . . . ."

"You're expecting someone to arrive tomorrow?"

She ran her tongue over her dry, unpainted lips.

"Someone to arrive? I wonder. If anyone could tell
me what's going to happen tomorrow."

She got up as heavily as an old woman.

"I'll go and tell Madame Ruby to see about your
seat in the train. Marguerite will help you with your
packing."

"Or Lucie. She knows where I keep all my things."

The unhappy, tear-washed elderly woman reared herself up straight. Flushed and sparkling with anger, she looked suddenly young again.

"Terribly sorry. Lucie's not there. Lucie's through!"

"She's leaving you?"

"Leaving *me*? Considering I've thrown *her* out, the slut! There are . . . interesting conditions that I find very far from interesting! Really, the things one has to put up with in this world!"

She went off down the muddy path, her white skirt held up in both hands. I did not linger to consider the scattered wreckage at my feet, the work of the civilized monster masquerading in human shape, the creature who lusted to kill birds.

Madame Suzanne did everything possible to satisfy my keen and slightly cowardly desire to leave Bella-Vista that very day. She did not forget Pati's ticket and insisted on accompanying me to the train. Dressed in tight-fitting black, she sat beside me on the back seat, and all through the drive, she preserved a stiffness which was equally suitable to a well-to-do businesswoman or a proud creature going to the scaffold. In front of us was Madame Ruby's erect, T-shaped torso and her handsome head with its rakishly tilted beret.

At the station, I managed to persuade Madame Suzanne to stay in the car. My last sight of her was behind the windows misted with fine rain. It was Madame Ruby who carried my heaviest suitcase, bought me papers, and settled me in my carriage with the greatest possible friendliness.

But I received these attentions somewhat ungraciously. I had an unjust feeling which refused to admit that this easy assurance quite caught the manner of a masculine female, adept at making women blush under her searching glances. I was on the verge of reproaching myself for ever having been taken in by this tough fellow whose walk, whose whole appearance was that of an old Irish sergeant who had dressed himself up as a woman for a joke on St. Patrick's Day.